Kate Greenaway's

Mother

Goose

Huntington Library
San Marino, California

Published by Huntington Library Press
1151 Oxford Road
San Marino, CA 91108 USA
www.huntington.org

ISBN-10: 0-87328-216-7
ISBN-13: 978-0-87328-216-1

INTRODUCTION

FOR MANY GENERATIONS, Mother Goose has been a common heritage for all children who have known nursery rhymes and for all parents who have read or recited them to children. Other nursery rhymes there may be, but those in the collections called *Mother Goose* have enjoyed the status of classics. The vividness with which we remember our *Mother Goose* depends a lot on the illustrations. Among the illustrators, Kate Greenaway stands at the top: no one has ever equaled the artistic quality and the appeal of her drawings. It is a special pleasure to offer, in facsimile, this selection of Kate Greenaway's illustrations to *Mother Goose,* from the rare first edition of 1881 in the Huntington Library. It will, I hope, be a treat for younger people and older people alike, either as a revival of happy memories or as a discovery of new pleasures.

Kate Greenaway was thirty-five years old when her *Mother Goose* was published. Trained as an artist, she was already a professional illustrator of note, and she attracted a wide audience. Her characteristic style, which made a deep impact on such a discerning critic as John Ruskin, revolutionized the art of book illustration. Her drawings still seem fresh, with clear outlines, distinctive colors, and graceful action; a Pre-Raphaelite spirit runs through her work.

The appeal of her drawings reflects her real interest in children, in flowers, in houses, and in her preoccupation with a state of innocence in which people have big round eyes and open faces. Her bond of sympathy draws us to Jack and Jill, to the dispirited ten o'clock scholar, and to her whole range of boys and girls. Despite her interest in children, she never married.

She chose to costume her characters in the long dresses, bonnets, and trousers of a style that had been popular almost a century in the past, about the year 1800. (The present revival of interest in Kate Greenaway must have something to do with the fact that long dresses on little girls seem less uncommon now than they did a generation ago.) She intended her choice of clothes from an earlier age to create an old-fashioned, rather quaint look that would encourage her Victorian contemporaries to enjoy her gentle humor, and the amusement is there for us too.

Kate Greenaway's versions of nursery rhymes are those she learned as a child in London and in Nottingham-shire, and some of them will strike our ears as odd. Almost everybody thinks that the versions of his own childhood are the true ones, but the fact is that nursery rhymes—like most verses passed on orally—vary among countries, in parts of a country, and in different times. What we call nursery rhymes were not, for the most part, written for children; they were taken over from adult literature and adapted into a nursery rhyme form, in which repetition and swinging cadence outrun meaning. Nursery rhymes are usually part of an oral tradition long before they ever appear in print.

"Mother Goose," as a title for a printed collection of nursery rhymes, originated in the middle of the eighteenth century, in England. It quickly made its way to this country, where it has survived better than in England. "Mother Goose" came from a French title for prose fairy tales of the latter seventeenth century; despite legends to the contrary, there does not seem to have been any real person who was the original Mother Goose.

The Huntington Library, a major repository of materials for the study of English and American literature and history, has a rich collection of books illustrated by Kate Greenaway, as well as a few of her manuscripts; almost a hundred of her original drawings are in the Art Collection. I hope that this little book, a small example from a large collection, will convey some of the charm of her work.

James Thorpe

·MOTHER GOOSE·

MOTHER GOOSE
or the
OLD NURSERY RHYMES

Illustrated by
· KATE GREENAWAY ·

engraved and
printed by
○ EDMUND EVANS ○

London and New York:
George Routledge and Sons.

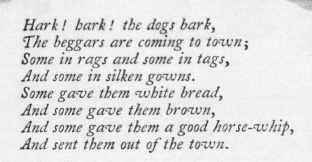

Hark! hark! the dogs bark,
The beggars are coming to town;
Some in rags and some in tags,
And some in silken gowns.
Some gave them white bread,
And some gave them brown,
And some gave them a good horse-whip,
And sent them out of the town.

K.G.

5

Little Jack Horner, sat in the corner,
Eating a Christmas pie;
He put in his thumb, and pulled out a plum,
And said, oh! what a good boy am I.

There was an old woman
Lived under a hill;
And if she's not gone,
She lives there still.

Diddlty, diddlty, dumpty,
The cat run up the plum tree;
Give her a plum, and down she'll come,
Diddlty, diddlty, dumpty.

K.G

We're all jolly boys, and we're coming
        with a noise,
Our stockings shall be made
Of the finest silk,
And our tails shall touch the ground.

K.G.

9

To market, to market, to buy a plum cake,
Home again, home again, market is late;
To market, to market, to buy a plum bun,
Home again, home again, market is done.

Elsie Marley has grown so fine,
She won't get up to serve the swine;
But lies in bed till eight or nine,
And surely she does take her time.

II

Daffy-down-dilly has come up to town,
In a yellow petticoat and a green gown.

K.d

Jack Sprat could eat no fat,
His wife could eat no lean;
And so between them both,
They licked the platter clean.

K.G.

Lucy Locket, lost her pocket,
Kitty Fisher found it;
There was not a penny in it,
But a ribbon round it.

KG

Cross Patch, lift the latch,
Sit by the fire and spin;
Take a cup, and drink it up,
Then call your neighbours in.

Johnny shall have a new bonnet,
And Johnny shall go to the fair;
And Johnny shall have a blue ribbon,
To tie up his bonny brown hair.

K.G

There was a little boy and a little girl
Lived in an alley;
Says the little boy to the little girl,
"Shall I, oh! shall I?"
Says the little girl to the little boy,
"What shall we do?"
Says the little boy to the little girl,
"I will kiss you!"

K.G.

Draw a pail of water,
For my lady's daughter;
My father's a king, and my mother's a queen,
My two little sisters are dressed in green,
Stamping grass and parsley,
Marigold leaves and daisies.
One rush! two rush!
Pray thee, fine lady, come under my bush.

KG

Jack and Jill
Went up the hill,
To fetch a pail of water;
Jack fell down
And broke his crown,
And Jill came tumbling after.

K.G

19

Little Bo-peep has lost her sheep,
And can't tell where to find them;
Leave them alone, and they'll come home,
And bring their tails behind them.

Polly put the kettle on,
Polly put the kettle on,
Polly put the kettle on,
We'll all have tea.
Sukey take it off again,
Sukey take it off again,
Sukey take it off again,
They're all gone away.

Little Tommy Tittlemouse,
Lived in a little house;
He caught fishes
In other men's ditches.

Tell Tale Tit,
Your tongue shall be slit;
And all the dogs in the town
Shall have a little bit.

23

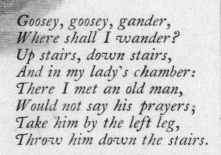

Goosey, goosey, gander,
Where shall I wander?
Up stairs, down stairs,
And in my lady's chamber:
There I met an old man,
Would not say his prayers;
Take him by the left leg,
Throw him down the stairs.

K.G

24

Willy boy, Willy boy, where are you going?
I will go with you, if I may.
I'm going to the meadow to see them a
        mowing,
I'm going to help them make the hay.

K.G.

Mary, Mary, quite contrary,
How does your garden grow?
With silver bells, and cockle shells,
And cowslips all of a row.

K.G

Bonny lass, pretty lass, wilt thou be mine?
Thou shalt not wash dishes,
Nor yet serve the swine;
Thou shalt sit on a cushion, and sew a
      fine seam,
And thou shalt eat strawberries, sugar,
      and cream!

A diller, a dollar,
A ten o'clock scholar;
What makes you come so soon?
You used to come at ten o'clock,
But now you come at noon!

KG

Little Betty Blue,
Lost her holiday shoe.
What will poor Betty do?
Why, give her another,
To match the other,
And then she will walk in two.

Billy boy blue, come blow me your horn,
The sheeps' in the meadow, the cows'
    in the corn;
Is that the way you mind your sheep,
Under the Haycock fast asleep?

Girls and boys come out to play,
The moon it shines, as bright as day;
Leave your supper, and leave your sleep,
And come to your playmates in the street;
Come with a whoop, come with a call,
Come with a good will, or come not at all;
Up the ladder and down the wall,
A halfpenny loaf will serve us all.

Here am I, little jumping Joan,
When nobody's with me,
I'm always alone.

Ride a cock-horse,
To Banbury-cross,
To see little Johnny
Get on a white horse.

K.G

33

D

Rock-a-bye baby,
Thy cradle is green;
Father's a nobleman,
Mother's a queen.
And Betty's a lady,
And wears a gold ring;
And Johnny's a drummer,
And drums for the king.

Little Tom Tucker,
He sang for his supper.
What did he sing for?
Why, white bread and butter.
How can I cut it without a knife?
How can I marry without a wife?

Little Miss Muffet,
Sat on a tuffet,
Eating some curds and whey;
There came a great spider,
And sat down beside her,
And frightened Miss Muffet away.

K.G

Humpty Dumpty sat on a wall,
Humpty Dumpty had a great fall.

K.G.

See-Saw-Jack in the hedge,
Which is the way to London-bridge?

Little lad, little lad,
Where wast thou born?
Far off in Lancashire,
Under a thorn;
Where they sup sour milk
From a ram's horn.

As I was going up Pippin Hill,
Pippin Hill was dirty;
There I met a sweet pretty lass,
And she dropped me a curtsey.

KG.

Little maid, little maid,
Whither goest thou?
Down in the meadow
To milk my cow.

My mother, and your mother,
Went over the way;
Said my mother, to your mother,
"It's chop-a-nose day."

K.G.

All around the green gravel,
The grass grows so green,
And all the pretty maids are fit to be seen;
Wash them in milk,
Dress them in silk,
And the first to go down shall be married.

One foot up, the other foot down,
That's the way to London-town.

K.G

Georgie Peorgie, pudding and pie,
Kissed the girls and made them cry;
When the girls begin to play,
Georgie Peorgie runs away.

As Tommy Snooks, and Bessie Brooks
Were walking out one Sunday;
Says Tommy Snooks to Bessie Brooks,
"To-morrow—will be Monday."

Tom, Tom, the piper's son,
He learnt to play when he was young,
He with his pipe made such a noise,
That he pleased all the girls and boys.

K.G

47

Ring-a-ring-a-roses,
A pocket full of posies;
Hush! hush! hush! hush!
We're all tumbled down.

48

DATE DUE

			PRINTED IN U.S.A.